Surprise
in the
Meadow

ANNA VOJTECH

Holiday House / New York

For Frida

Library of Congress Cataloging-in-Publication Data

Vojtech, Anna, author, illustrator.
Surprise in the meadow / Anna Vojtech. — First edition.
pages cm
Summary: The seeds Chipmunk buried last fall are missing, but in their place a beautiful sunflower grows
and by summer's end, drops its seeds for Chipmunk and the other creatures in the meadow to enjoy.
ISBN 978-0-8234-3556-2 (hardcover)
[1. Chipmunks—Fiction. 2. Sunflowers—Fiction. 3. Seeds—Fiction.] I. Title.
PZ7.1.V67Su 2016
[E]—dc23
2015019725

Spring had come to the meadow.

Little Chipmunk woke from his long winter sleep. He was hungry. He remembered the seeds he buried last fall. They had been so delicious!

Little Chipmunk went to his hiding place, but he found no seeds—only the shoot of a mysterious plant. His seeds had disappeared!

The spring sun was warm.

The mysterious shoot grew taller and taller.

The plant continued
to grow and grow.
Bigger than bluebell.
Bigger than
black-eyed Susan.
Even bigger than
Queen Anne's lace.

As the summer grew hotter,
the stream dried up. The grass
yellowed, and the flowers wilted.

Suddenly, the sky grew dark.

Splash! A drop fell. And another and another!
It rained all day and all night.

The stream filled, the grass
was green and the flowers
were beautiful again.
The big plant had a gigantic
golden flower, shining like the sun.

"Sunflower!" Little Chipmunk called.

Soon the meadow grew cool and crisp.
Fall was coming.
Little Chipmunk gathered food
for the winter.
The sunflower's head changed
from brilliant yellow to a brown
that darkened every day.

One blustery afternoon, a strong wind
blew through the meadow, shaking the
sunflower from side to side.
Little Chipmunk watched a brown
hailstorm coming down from the
sunflower's head.

When the wind settled, beneath
the sunflower Little Chipmunk found
hundreds of brown seeds. He bit into
one. It tasted just like the seeds he
had been looking for in the spring.
His seeds had not disappeared after all!
He buried some of the seeds
and filled his belly with
the rest for the long
winter ahead.

Life Cycle of a Sunflower

A sunflower starts as a tiny seed buried in the ground.

Roots grow down from the seed into the soil.

A shoot grows up from the seed.

Leaves grow from the shoot. The shoot grows stronger and straighter and becomes a stem, then a sturdy stalk.

A sunflower needs nutrients from the soil, air, water and sunlight to grow. It can grow more than ten feet tall.

A bud grows at the top of the plant. It opens into a flower head with yellow ray flowers around the edge and hundreds of small disk flowers in the middle.

The ray flowers attract bees. The bees pollinate the disk flowers, which then produce seeds.

The seeds ripen. They turn brown.

In autumn, the sunflower withers and dies. The seeds fall to the ground. Some are blown away by the wind; some are eaten by birds, mice, deer and raccoons and by squirrels and chipmunks, who also bury seeds in the ground.